n

The Chronicle

Published in the United States of America by The Child's World®
1980 Lookout Drive • Mankato, MN 56003-1705
800-599-READ • www.childsworld.com

ACKNOWLEDGMENTS
The Child's World®: Mary Berendes, Publishing Director
The Design Lab: Kathleen Petelinsek, Design and Page Production
Literacy Consultants: Cecilia Minden, PhD, and Joanne Meier, PhD

LIBRARY OF CONGRESS
CATALOGING-IN-PUBLICATION DATA
Moncure, Jane Belk.
  My "n" sound box / by Jane Belk Moncure ;
illustrated by Rebecca Thornburgh.
    p. cm. — (Sound box books)
  Summary: "Little n has an adventure with items beginning with
her letter's sound, such as nickels, a necklace, and nine nesting
nightingales eating nuts."—Provided by publisher.
  ISBN 978-1-60253-154-3 (library bound : alk. paper)
  [1. Alphabet.] I. Thornburgh, Rebecca McKillip, ill. II. Title. III.
Series.
  PZ7.M739Myn 2009
  [E]—dc22   2008033170

A NOTE TO PARENTS AND EDUCATORS:

Magic moon machines and five fat frogs are just a few of the fun things you can share with children by reading books with them. Reading aloud helps children in so many ways! It introduces them to new words, motivates them to develop their own reading skills, and expands their attention span and listening abilities. So it's important to find time each day to share a book or two . . . or three!

As you read with young children, you can help develop their understanding of how print works by talking about the parts of the book—the cover, the title, the illustrations, and the words that tell the story. As you read, use your finger to point to each word, modeling a gentle sweep from left to right.

Simple word games help develop important prereading skills, including an understanding of rhyme and alliteration (when words share the same beginning sound, such as "six" and "sand"). Try playing with words from a book you've just shared: "What other words start with the same sound as moon?" "Cat and hat, do those words rhyme?" The possibilities are endless—and so are the rewards!

My "n" Sound Box®

WRITTEN BY JANE BELK MONCURE

ILLUSTRATED BY REBECCA THORNBURGH

Little  had a box. "I will find

things that begin with my

n sound," she said. "I will put

them into my sound box."

Little  found a tree with

nuts on it.

Little  climbed the tree. She picked nuts. How many nuts?

Little 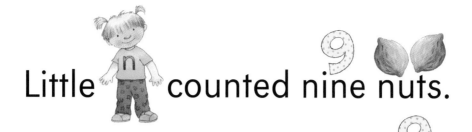 counted nine nuts.

She made the number nine.

Did she put the nuts and the
number nine into her box? She did.

Next, Little  made nine groups of nuts. How many nuts in all?

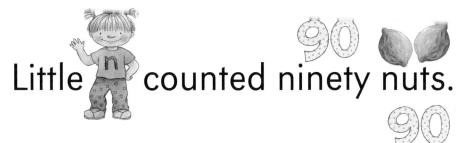

Little **n** counted ninety nuts.

She made the number ninety.

She put these nuts into her box

with the other nuts. Now how

many nuts did she have? Little

counted ninety-nine nuts.

She made the number ninety-nine.

Did she put the number ninety-nine

into her box? She did.

Then Little  climbed the

tree again.

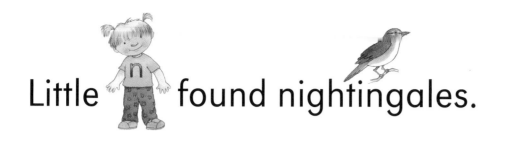 Little n found nightingales.

She found nine nightingales
eating nuts!

When the nightingales saw Little , they flew into their nests.

Little  put the nightingales and their nests into her box. She was careful because there were eggs in the nests.

Little 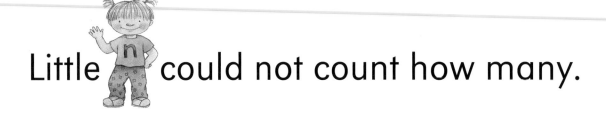 could not count how many.

Little 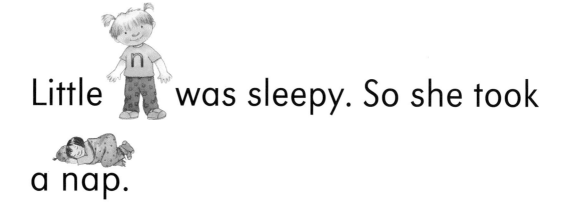 was sleepy. So she took
a nap.

The next day, Little  got out

her piggy bank.

She emptied out her nickels.

There were ninety-nine nickels!

Little 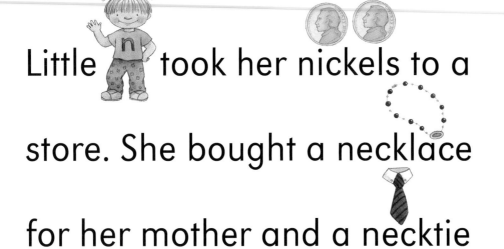 took her nickels to a store. She bought a necklace for her mother and a necktie for her father. She also bought a nutcracker.

Little  had nineteen nickels left. So she bought a nightgown for herself.

Little carried all her new

things home. She put on her

new nightgown.

Then she heard a noise. She

looked into her box and saw

19 nineteen new nightingales.

They were crying for nuts!

"Don't cry," said Little . "I have  enough nuts for all of you." She  cracked some nuts.

While the nightingales ate, she

spread out her new things.

Little  n's Word List

nap

necklace

necktie

nest

nickel

nightgown

nightingale

nine 9

nineteen 19

ninety 90

ninety-nine 99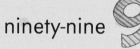

numbers 123

nut

nutcracker

28

Other Words with Little

nail

newspaper

notes

napkin

noodles

November

neck

nose

nurse

net

notebook

More to Do!

Little **n** had fun counting nightingales, nuts, and nickels. Now it's your turn!

Directions:

1. Draw a simple table like the one below.

Item	Guess	Actual
Raisins		
Paper clips		
Blocks		
Crayons		
Pennies		
Your own idea!		

2. Grab a handful of the first item listed in the first column. Guess how many you have in your hand. Write that number in the "Guess" column.

3. Count how many items you actually had in your hand. Write that number in the "Actual" column.

4. Now move on to the second item on the list. Repeat steps 2 and 3 for this item. Keep repeating steps 2 and 3 for all of the items on your list.

5. How close were your guesses? Was it harder to come close to the actual number with bigger items or smaller items? Why?

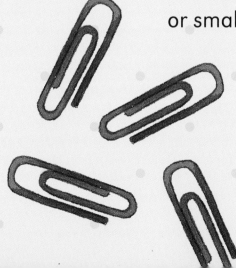

About the Author

Best-selling author Jane Belk Moncure has written over 300 books throughout her teaching and writing career. After earning a Master's degree in Early Childhood Education from Columbia University, she became one of the pioneers in that field. In 1956, she helped form the Virginia Association for Early Childhood Education, which established the first statewide standards for teachers of young children.

Inspired by her work in the classroom, Mrs. Moncure's books have become standards in primary education, and her name is recognized across the country. Her success is reflected not only in her books' popularity with parents, children, and educators, but also by numerous awards, including the 1984 C. S. Lewis Gold Medal Award.

About the Illustrator

Rebecca Thornburgh lives in a pleasantly spooky old house in Philadelphia. If she's not at her drawing table, she's reading—or singing with her band, called Reckless Amateurs. Rebecca has one husband, two daughters, and two silly dogs.